A step into The Siren's Call

Tammy Bradley

Copyright © 2023 Tammy Bradley

All rights reserved

The characters and events portrayed in this book are fictitious. Any similarity to real persons, living or dead, is coincidental and not intended by the author.

No part of this book may be reproduced, or stored in a retrieval system, or transmitted in any form or by any means, electronic, mechanical, photocopying, recording, or otherwise, without express written permission of the publisher.

ISBN: 9798288242335

www.authortammybradley.com

Content Warnings

This book is strictly for readers over the age of eighteen, the content is also not for the faint hearted. It has graphically explained sex scenes, sex acts which also have BDSM aspects and blood play.

The book is set in a mafia world, so violence, torture and killings are throughout.

My main male character can be dominant, grumpy and an Alphahole by nature. My main female characters are feisty, strong but also have submissive tendencies in the bedroom. They can be territorial, aggressive, jealous and controlling, sometimes overly so.

I have graphic torture scenes, kidnapping, knife play and fight scenes. Characters are also killed or wounded.

There is also graphic language throughout this book.

If any of these things offend you in any way, please do not read on, I am also probably not the author for you as this is the style of the dark romance I write.

My book is also written in British-English.

If none of the above has bothered you, welcome to my dark world of romance. I hope you enjoy my book and look forward to hearing what you think about it if you leave a review.

Acknowledgments

Firstly, I'd like to thank my Fiancé Craig; none of this would have been possible without you. You taught me I was able to love and be loved. You also gave me the support and confidence to finally chase my dreams.

I had kept my love of writing a secret from everyone, with no confidence and a low self-esteem. Even you didn't know I dreamt of being a writer until 25 years later. Yes, I know that was a big shock to everyone including you.

Our life together has been full of beautiful memories, love, and hope. But then we had the biggest tragedy any parent could have. We lost our beloved daughter Lexi. We cried, we broke, and we both very nearly didn't make it through. We have now come to the realisation that we will always be broken and none of our pieces will ever be put back together.

We have learned to adapt and live life for our 3 other precious daughters. They saved us with their smiles, love, and altogether craziness.

Thank you, Craig, for giving me 4 gorgeous girls,

love and a home. Our story was never meant to be a bed of roses fairy tale. We were meant to be the hard-ass survivors who get to the end of our story with scars, bruises and bad hair.

I'm looking forward to the future with you and the girls. Our happily ever after is waiting for us, nobody can ever take that away from us. It's you and me until the end babe, love you forever and always.

To my children, my crazy girlies. I hope you are proud of your Momma even though you will probably never be allowed to read my books! I love you all more than life itself.

You saved me when I thought there was no hope when we lost Lexi. You showed me my biggest battle still lay ahead and gave me the strength to carry on.

I don't know what I did to deserve you all, but I thank the Gods for you every day. I'm never going to win any awards for best Mom, but know this my beautiful girlies. I will always love you with all my heart and soul.

You make me so proud. I hope all of your dreams and ambitions for your own futures come true. I'll be with you every step of the way.

To my precious Angel Lexi, I miss you so much every day my sweet angel, that it hurts to breathe. I know I was being unfair when I was begging for you to stay, I just didn't want you to be somewhere that I knew I couldn't follow.

Though your life was only a few short years on this earth, you showed me what it's like to witness a true-life warrior. You fought so hard, defeated minimal odds, and always had a smile on your face while doing it. Oh, unless you had a nummy in your mouth or were snuggled in a blanket sleeping.

I was blessed to have you as my beautiful daughter and experience a life enriched by you. You were too precious for this earth. You had a far more important journey to fulfil. Your wings were ready, but Momma's heart wasn't!

Fly high sweet angel, fly high. Until we meet again, all my love always, Mom x

To my mom, what can I say Mom, but our journey has definitely been interesting. I hope I have been able to make you proud and I will always love you. Look after my Angel when it's time and make sure she knows how much I love her every day. You may have been called early but it's just your time to look after more than just us. You now have a higher purpose so do us proud.

Now, to my dear friends, that I've found along the way.

Kerry Morgan, my fellow nutter, PA, cheerleader and dearest friend. Thank you for all your support and patience with me whilst I was writing this book. You picked me up if I fell and kicked my arse when I doubted myself. Keep being you beautiful and I can't wait to read your first book when it's out. Love you babe.

Fiona Ferguson, you are an amazing friend and how much we have in common is scary. I'm so glad I met you and brought you to the Dark side. Keep smiling beautiful, and I love you.

Maggie Brown, Annalee Adams, Ashlie-Louise Pearson and Alyssha Glenn, I love you all dearly and thank you so much for everything you have done for me. You are always there when I need you and help me at the drop of a hat. My angel definitely sent you my way.

Open Eye Editing my Editors, who under a very restricted deadline edited and polished my book to perfection. I cannot thank you enough for everything you have done for me, and I look forward to working with you again on book 2.

My Alpha team, Kerry Morgan, Sharon Jackson and Raluca Butusina. To my Beta team and Arc team you are truly fantastic, thank you all for your help and support.

I'd lastly like to thank my fans for reading my books. Without you, I would never have been able to achieve my dreams. Thank you so much for all your love and support.

Chapter 1

Annabelle

Kim comes over and pinches my eyeliner as I touch up my Cherry Red lipstick.

"For fuck's sake Kim, that was new today, you better give me that back when you're done bitch. You're always running off with my stuff and never giving it back!" I scowl at her in the mirror and go back to add another layer of mascara.

"Chill your tits Belle, I'll give it back to you in a bit. What crawled up your arse today anyway?" Kim says, as she walks back to her dressing table in a black lacy thong. I think I've seen more of her body than the guests at the club have, but hey, this is what comes with dancing at a burlesque club I guess.

"I'm just pissed off with having to buy new stuff all the time because you pinch it! Remember to put it back this time." I look myself over and fluff my hair up more, giving it extra volume that it doesn't need. I see Kim flip me off in my mirror and smile back at her.

Rose stands up from her own dresser and walks over to me. She's gorgeous, a tall platinum blonde, with a figure to die for and a huge pair of boobs. I've only been here for a short time, four months to be precise, but I would consider Rose one of my closest friends. I've missed having female friends.

"Are you okay Belle? You seem nervous tonight and that's unusual for you!" She puts her hand on my shoulder trying to comfort me.

"I'm just a bit on edge... as Pete said earlier the owner is in tonight!" I've never met the owner of the Club, as it was Pete the manager who hired me.

"Oh sweetie, don't worry about Kai! He'll be too busy in meetings or with some slut in the VIP lounge," she said, walking off to finish getting into her next outfit.

Everyone here is nice, but only if you don't get in their way of making money. A few of the girls are a bit upset though because I've been given the lucrative spotlight dance for the past two weeks.

We've already done four burlesque group routines tonight, then my spotlight freestyle and Crystal's pole dance, followed by some of the other girls' performances. My upcoming routine is my last dance of the night.

With a small sigh I get up to put on the costume for my dance. I had to be on stage in about ten minutes.

I ran my hands over the outfit rail; all feathers, sequins and barely there ensembles.

I picked out my black lace see-through teddy that, as you can imagine, showed more of my body than it hid. Only my pussy was hidden by the elaborate ivy embroidered across it. I added thigh-high stockings and a pair of black stiletto heels. The finishing touch was my black lace gloves, and I was ready to go.

It didn't bother me to show my body off, as this was my way of rebelling against the life I'd been born into. This was my choice and if they didn't like it? Well; they could fuck off.

Dancing is my life. I've loved it from such a young age, even going to dance school three times a week. I fully intended to commit to it more if I was allowed, and eventually teach. Unfortunately, life took a vastly different turn at seventeen proving my life thus far was full of lies, deceit and betrayal. Shaking myself, I thought, 'enough of that.' The past is never a good place to go.

Sam, who looks after the dancers and is a regular mother hen to all of us, comes rushing in. She's stunning, with black hair and striking pale blue eyes. She used to dance, but then took to looking after the girls when she had a little girl about two years ago. So instead, she orders or makes all our costumes and does the set order every week.

"Belle you're up sweetie, it's packed out there! Show them what you're made of!" She gives me her megawatt smile and rushes off backstage. I take a deep breath and make my own way backstage to take my spot.

I stand there with my back to the curtains, right leg extended out and my hands clasped together in the air. The familiar sound of the curtains opening draws my attention to the audience. I have a quick peek and I've never seen it so full. The spotlight blinks to life and the audience disappears behind the glare. As the first bars of 'Under the influence' by Chris Brown spills out of the speakers, I take a breath and start to dance.

Running my hand down my left arm that is still suspended in the air, I shift my weight over to my right side and bend, gliding a hand up the length of my leg, giving everyone in the audience a generous view of my arse in the teddy thong. Lifting myself gracefully upright I spiral into a pirouette, turning to face the audience. Face down, my flaming red hair cascades down in waves to cover it.

The guys go crazy, calling out to me, whistling and cheering like an ocean roaring. I stand feet apart and lift my head slowly.

I continue on with my routine letting the music carry me away, falling into the beat, running my hands over myself, allowing it to consume me. The tempo takes over my body as I lose myself to the dance.

The stage is wide and I walk gracefully over to

the runway at its centre, which leads out into the middle of the club. Strolling seductively, I make my way down it, stopping halfway before dropping to my knees. Tipping my head back I begin rotating my hips, undulating them smoothly and, with each rotation, I open my knees. Dropping my bottom to the floor as though I'm riding a man, caressing my body with wandering hands. My hair brushes the curve of my arse in a sinful tease. Running my hands back up my body, I caress my breasts and move up to my throat.

As I'm lost in melodic ecstasy, a buzz of electricity sparks and prickles along my skin. I raise my head slowly and lock eyes with the most piercing ocean-blue eyes I've ever seen. The sight steals my breath. The spotlight isn't as bright here so I can see him fully.

Surveying the scene, I see he's sitting in the VIP lounge and his heated stare has me pinned. Captured by it, unable to tear my eyes away, I run my hands back over my body as I lower myself onto all fours and crawl further in his direction. Letting my gaze roam over him I finally notice the blonde, her face buried in his lap, giving him enthusiastic head. His hand is on the back of her head, pushing her down further on his cock at a rapid pace as I crawl toward him.

Bringing my gaze back to his, I find he hasn't looked away as he raises a mocking eyebrow at me.

Stopping at the end of the runway, directly in front of him, I quickly decided to answer his silent challenge. Let's see how long he lasts if I up the ante. I move to the beat once again; dropping my top half to the floor, I open my legs wider. Keeping my arse in the air, I pulse it up and down in a humping motion. In response he grabs the blonde's head on both sides and matches my movements. The audience is forgotten; I can't take my eyes off him. I'm enraptured in our game.

Rolling to my back, eyes on his, I tilt my head off the stage. Holding my legs pressed together, I lift them straight up in the air before spreading them wide. I repeat this a few times slowly, gradually easing them down to the floor again. Raising my knees I open them widely, caressing my hands over my breasts, while my hips are swivelling and thrusting to the music. Keeping my left hand on my breast I let my right hand roam down my body to my pussy. Rubbing over it a few times, I catch my clit which is throbbing for attention. Why is this man turning me on so much?

I lower my arse to the floor and flip onto my front. Easing back into the kneeling position, I spread my knees out wide. Bringing my fingers to my mouth tauntingly, my left hand goes back to my breast caressing it teasingly.

He stops his ministrations for a few seconds, gritting his teeth, and I know he's close. His pupils are dilated as his intense stare focuses on me and only me. I smile salaciously, putting two laced fingers in my mouth and sucking hard before removing them, placing my hand to my pussy yet again.

I gyrate against them, not quite touching, mimicking getting myself off right in front of him as I get lost once again in the music. He resumes his own rhythm to match mine as we clash in a battle of wills and lust. We both get more frenzied with our movements.

I'm not touching myself, but the intensity of the connection between us makes me feel like I want to come. The song is nearing its end and I know the moment will soon be lost.

His teeth grind down and his jaw strains, his hand presses the blonde's head hard to his lap and holds it there. His mouth opens and he tilts his head slightly back, his eyes never leaving mine. He tenses and I know he's coming; I throw my head back and tremble with need. Making it appear as if I too am in the throes of an orgasm.

The music stops and I lower my gaze to the floor, breaking the spell. Pushing myself up I pay him no attention, and turn my back, adding extra sway to my step as I sashay back to the main stage. Turning away, the audience goes wild. I let myself have one last look, and as he meets me with his own, I blow him a kiss and exit the stage out of view.

The adulation of the crowd follows behind me and

I lean against the wall, my heart thundering in my chest as I try to compose myself. What the hell was I thinking? *Jesus Belle what the fuck.* My body is so hot and I'm so bloody horny it's unbelievable. *Get a grip, Belle!* I try to tell myself as I make my way back to the dressing rooms.

Sitting down at my dresser I take a few deep breaths of relief. Sam rushes in and calls to me.

"Belle, I don't know what the hell you just did on that stage, but the audience hasn't shut up yet. Bloody hell girl, you didn't dance it like that in rehearsal! My God I think I have a girl crush on you myself!" She starts fanning herself and I can't help but laugh.

We're both laughing when Adonis walks through the door, right into our dressing rooms. He looks directly at me and I start to feel a bit worried. He strolls over to us.

"The boss wants to speak to Little Red here!" he says to Sam, then looks at me.

"Of course, I'll send her over when she's dressed, Lev," Sam says, to which Lev leaves the room. I look at Sam with wide eyes, *what the hell would he want with me?*

"Get dressed quickly Belle and make sure you wear a nice dress from the rack. You don't want to keep Kai waiting!" Sam rushes out of the room. I quickly freshened up and chose a figure-hugging emerald silk dress with a high split to wear. I hesitantly walk out of the dressing room to meet up with Sam and find out my fate.

Kai

What a shit show today has been. Two shipments have been delayed and I can't get the answers. I need to find out why. This enrages me so I sent Misha and Pasha to sort it out because, if I go myself, I will end up killing them all with the mood I'm in. Add this to the meeting I've just had with one of my associates, which ended in me grabbing him around the throat and throwing him over the table to kick the shit out of him. Well, I'd say today has been a total shit show of a day.

"Do you want me to let the girl in Kai?" Lev asks from behind me in the VIP lounge of my club. I thought having the meeting here would have been a good idea but now, sitting in The Siren's Call- my burlesque club, I'm second-guessing my decisions.

"Send her in." I don't look around as I answer Lev, instead I continue to look at the stage, watching the show as the girls do their routine. A whiff of cheap perfume hits my senses and I already know this day is beyond saving. Suddenly Amy stands right in front of my view and goes to touch my face. I grab her wrist and squeeze it hard.

"You know what to do, now fucking kneel and get the fuck on with it!" Amy pouts but kneels and starts undoing my belt and pulling down my fly. My erection springs free, but it's going down by the second.

Amy starts to pump my cock and caress my balls. Which just fucking annoys me. I want to call an end to it, but I need to get off. I sit up and whip my belt off, grabbing Amy's hands and pinning them behind her back. I wrap my belt around them and fasten it in place so she can't use her hands on me again.

"Get my fucking cock in your mouth and stop pissing about," I spit with venom, lifting my cock and forcing it into her mouth. She looks at me with doe eyes, thinking I'm going to take pity on her. Fuck that! She's just a mouth to fuck. If she doesn't want to do it properly, I'll find someone that does.

She goes to town, trying to get my cock interested but it's at half-mast now and going down by the second. I put my hand on the back of her head and forced her down further, hitting the back of her throat. She gags and my cock finally pays attention. I keep on forcing her up and down on my cock.

I glance at the stage for inspiration. The curtains are just opening and the vision I see before me is mesmerising. A petite redhead stands with her back to us. She's in nothing but underwear and killer heels. Her red wavy locks hang temptingly down her back, nearly reaching to her voluptuous arse as the thong of her outfit disappears between her cheeks. She starts dancing and bends over to caress her hand from her feet upwards.

My cock goes rock fucking hard in seconds as I'm

faced with her arse on full display. She stands and pirouettes to face me. Now I can see her lace-covered pussy begging for my attention. She has her head down, face covered by her hair so I can't see her features yet. My eyes rake down her breath-taking body starting with her ample lace-covered breasts. They are enticingly large for her frame. My eyes continue their leisurely journey, to her tiny waist and down to her voluptuous hips and thighs.

She has a perfect hourglass figure that I want to devour. I've not seen this girl here before, however, she will know who I am by the end of the night. Or my name is not Nikolai Filippov. If I want something I will have it, regardless of the repercussions. No one escapes me.

She lifts her head and I see the most beautiful sky-blue eyes I've ever seen. The little vixen continues with her routine, pressing nearer to me with every move. She's looking at everyone in the audience except for me, and it pisses me off. I keep moving Amy down on my cock, nearly forgetting that she needed to breathe.

The vixen on stage stops halfway and suddenly drops to her knees. She moves effortlessly and seems to let the music take control of her body. She tips her head back as she caresses her gorgeous body, and I can't fucking help it; I force Amy's head up and down on my cock imaging this Goddess on stage riding it instead.

I've never had a woman affect me like *this, ever*. I fuck them and get rid. I have no time for a woman. Never have, never will that's my number one rule. What the fuck is happening to me?

My Little Vixen on the stage brings her head back up and locks her eyes with mine. A shiver runs through my body and my cock's response is to thicken as my balls draw up. I'm so fucking turned on by this beauty that I know I will have to make her mine. That thought troubles me, so I choose to ignore it for now and go with the flow.

My Little Vixen looks down at my lap and watches me force Amy's head up and down on my engorged cock. Her eyes lock back with mine and I expect her to look away. But no, my vixen decides she wants to play, and the thrill that runs through my body is indescribable.

She comes to a stop right in front of me, at the end of the stage runway, continuing to dance erotically, her eyes never leaving mine. Dropping to the floor, she pushes her luscious tits into the stage with her delectable arse high in the air. Oh, how I want to get up on that stage and mark that arse with my hand. Maybe even with my belt. Fuck yeah, my stripes would look perfect on her porcelain skin. I'll bet I'll be able to see my marks on her for days.

Suddenly, she starts pumping her arse up and down like she's riding my cock again. I grab Amy's head, placing my hands on either side and pumping to the same rhythm as my vixen. Amy is gagging like hell, but do I give a fuck if she can't cope? Abso-fucking-lutely not. She can fuck right off.

My vixen flips over on her back and hangs her head over the stage, always keeping her eyes locked on mine. I wonder why she attracts my attention so much, as I always prefer a submissive by nature. One that would never dare to make eye contact and never push my boundaries like this little minx. I wonder if her brazenness is what is refreshing about her. Maybe? She carries on with her teasing and now she has her hand on her pussy, making me want to personally drag her off the stage.

My dominating nature is taking over now, and I want only my eyes to see her touching that pussy, making her get herself off before I clean up the mess she made with my tongue.

She's now on her knees, and I keep Amy's head steady on my cock. I'm ready to burst and I'm grinding my teeth to the point of pain. My vixen smiles at me and puts two lace-covered fingers in her mouth and sucks. I groan out loud before I can stop myself. The little minx is going to pay for that smile later. Amy moans for some fucking reason. I can bet she's happy with herself, thinking she's managed to get a reaction out of me because no woman ever has. What Amy will soon realise is that it's got fuck all to do with her.

My Little Vixen trails her wet fingers down to her

pussy and starts to slowly rub over it. I match her, moving Amy's head at the same pace and our little game continues. I keep pace with her as she quickens her movements and her little pink tongue comes out to wet her lips, making me groan again. I can see her panting and a delectable flush in her cheeks tells me she's as fucking turned on as I am.

I try to grit my teeth again knowing any second I'm going to blow, but it's useless. I push Amy's head fully down on my cock so I'm now down her throat and come like I've never done before. I can feel Amy struggling to breathe but I don't fucking care. I tilt my head back with my mouth open in euphoria, keeping my eyes on my vixen who has her head thrown back as she mimics her own orgasmic reaction.

I'm pissed because she's broken eye contact and I want her attention back on me. I crave it, which is so fucking foreign to me. She finishes her display but keeps her head down, her eyes on the floor. I sit up, willing her to look at me, but she turns her back and saunters back towards the curtains on stage.

Finally my vixen turns her head towards me, making eye contact again and blowing me a kiss as she walks off stage. What the actual fuck? This little minx is in a whole heap of trouble now, mark my words.

I push Amy off me, putting my still erect cock back into my trousers and fastening them. Amy starts to smile at me from the floor and I've had enough. I grab her hands and unfasten my belt from around them. I thread it through my trousers abruptly refastening it.

"Get the fuck out. I don't want to see you again!" I say venomously to her.

"But Kai, I made you feel good, didn't I?" Amy whines, looking up at me with a stricken look on her face.

"You did fuck all for me, you're so fucking useless. The Goddess on stage got me off. I SAID GET THE FUCK OUT!" I'm at the point that my rage will make itself known, but Lev acts before that can happen. He quickly removes a grovelling Amy from the floor and escorts her out of the room.

I run my hand through my hair and pace the room. *What the fuck just happened.* Lev comes back in, handing me a glass of vodka. I knock it back; it takes the edge off but it's not what I need right now.

"Go get me my redheaded vixen now Lev!" I bark. Lev smiles, going off to do as I wish.

I've known Lev all my life, he knows me better than I know myself. That is why he's my second in command and closest friend. He always gets the job done, but will express his concerns if he thinks I'm wrong… in private. He's priceless in our world. Loyalty always is.

I can't wait to get my Little Vixen in here and see

which of her personas she brings. Will she be the vixen she portrayed or a meek little submissive? I don't know which one excites me more but I'm about to find out.

Chapter 2

Annabelle

I find Sam at the bar knocking back a tequila shot. A nervous energy I have never seen before emanates from her. I sit down on the stool next to her and she asks for two more shots of tequila.

She slides one over to me and turns to face me, a worried look on her face. The dread in the pool of my stomach threatens to boil over and the flight or fight feeling I'm familiar with encompasses me.

I grab hold of the bar to keep myself steady, so I don't run out of here like a bat out of hell. This is the only place I've felt comfortable in for the first time in three years, and I'm determined to keep hold of my new life for as long as I can.

"Belle. Look sweetie, you need to be careful now, I wouldn't normally be bothered that someone has drawn the attention of Kai. Plenty have come and gone in that department, believe me. The thing is they never last and he rarely ever goes back more than once. Some girls get heartbroken thinking they could have been his and end up leaving or they just end up bitter and twisted. You my girl are something special and I could tell that from the first moment you walked in through that door. You see, you have a beautiful soul that shines through those gorgeous sky-blue eyes of yours. There are the shadows I see when you think nobody is watching. I know you have demons that you are running from Belle, and I will never ask you about them I promise. Believe me, I have my own demons and they are locked away never to escape. I just don't want to lose you honey, so please be careful with that beautiful heart of yours, yeah!"

I sit there gobsmacked, my mouth slightly open for a beat too long as Sam reaches out and puts two fingers under my chin, closing my mouth for me with a loving smile on her face.

Normally I would have alarm bells ringing in my ears and an urge to run home to Luka and be on the next plane out of here. I mean we've done it plenty of times before but here? Here feels like the home I've never had.

Also, even though Sam isn't that much older than me. She reminds me so much of my mother that it hurts sometimes. Mama was not only stunningly beautiful, but also very intelligent. Above all else though, she had the kindest soul to ever brighten this godforsaken world. And I'd had a front-row seat when her beautiful soul was obliterated from this life. I have a scar so deep in my soul that I don't ever think it will stop aching from the pain.

A STEP INTO THE SIREN'S CALL

I shake myself out of my thoughts, as I need to dig deep and reassure Sam that I'm tougher than I look.

"Sam, trust me, I'm fine, honestly. I'll go and see what Kai wants and come back out to see you before I go. Okay?" I tap her hand resting on the bar and go to leave, but she grabs my hand in a vice-like grip.

"Please be careful Belle, Kai is a very dangerous man!" She suddenly lets go of my hand and looks around in the mirrors of the bar to see if anybody overheard our conversation.

I feel like asking more about who Kai is but, with how edgy Sam is acting, I decide not to. You see, Sam doesn't know the sort of evil I've been subjected to in my life and hopefully, she never finds out.

"Please don't worry Sam, I won't be long I promise!" I get up from the bar and head over to the entrance for the VIP lounge.

I walk over to Greg and Peter who spot me and stand aside smiling at me. I give them my flirtiest smile back and wink at them as I saunter past. I head up the stairs and come face to face with Lev.

He's standing with another man, guarding the doorway that leads to the VIP lounge. When he sees me, his scowl turns into a panty-dropping smile that I'm sure impresses all the ladies. He's tall, very muscular and heavily tattooed from what I can see of the ink peeking from his unbuttoned shirt. Add gorgeous, and that smile to the equation, and I think my own pants might have just flown off, never to be seen again.

"Hello there Little Red!" he says, winking at me.

The other guard stands there like a silent sentinel at the door and I give him a once over. He's also well muscled and looks a little like a tank, with a mean looking edge to him. On closer inspection there is something else I can't quite determine. As I study his face, I realise what's holding my attention. His eyes. Although his demeanour is mean, his eyes are full of a sadness that calls to my own, so I address him.

"I don't think we've met Tank," I cajole amiably.

His stern expression flickers to amusement and back, so quickly I wasn't sure whether I had imagined it.

"This is Pasha," Lev chipped in.

"He doesn't say much, and he can be a mean sonofabitch," he adds.

Pasha inclines his head and steps to the side, allowing me access to the door.

"Are you ready to play with the big bad wolf today? Because my dear you have certainly riled him up good and proper!" Lev asks tauntingly.

I walk up to him and rest my hand on his chest, peering up at him through my lashes.

"Honey, I'll have him purring like a kitten by the time I'm out of here, so don't you worry that pretty little head of yours. Oh, and I might be small but don't underestimate this little pocket rocket! I like to bite!" I run my hand slightly down his chest and smirk at him before opening the door and entering the VIP lounge.

The VIP lounge is luxurious, lit with ambient blue lighting. Leather and plush velvet seating faces a balcony overlooking the entire club.

Kai stands with his back to me, his hands in his pockets as he looks over his kingdom. He's tall, blonde, 6ft5 at least and muscular if the pull of his shirt over his back is anything to go by.

His jacket is hanging over the back of a chair, discarded in favour of his sleeves rolled up to as far as they will go on his bulging forearms. The black silk shirt ripples across his body with every movement.

My attention is drawn to his glorious arse, oh my Lord I think I may be drooling. *'Oh my god woman, get a grip.'* I draw my attention away, with regret, from that peachy goodness and walk towards him.

"I believe you wanted to see me?" I say with my head held high and my shoulders back. *Come on Boss Man, let's continue our little game, let's see what you've got.*

"You, my Little Vixen, put on quite a show tonight. Pray, tell me was that all for my benefit? Did you want my attention, crave it maybe, or do you normally dance like that in my club?"

He isn't even looking at me and both that and his

comment have me riled. Right Mr, my claws are coming out!

"I dance like that all the time, in your club as you put it! But believe me when I say that I do not want or crave your attention, Boss Man! If I draw a man's attention that's his problem not mine, I'm just doing the job you pay me to do. I consider you to be quite rude though, as a poor blonde was choking on your cock at the time! Your attention should have remained with her!"

I'm lying. In a way I did crave his attention, but I would never admit to it, and I will not be seen as an attention-seeking whore. I do what I do for me, a rebellion against my past life. Two fingers up at all the men who have tried to dictate and rule my life so far. I'll be fucked if I'll let another man think he can rule me again.

"Oh, but you see my Little Vixen, the blonde was irritating the fuck out of me until you came out on my stage. She served her purpose, as I imagined you sucking my dick up here, instead of what you imitated on my stage. You might want to lie to yourself Little Vixen but understand this. Don't ever fucking lie to me again, as you will not like the consequences!"

I swear that steam is coming out of my ears because I'm that mad. How fucking dare he! He's so fucking up himself that he's high off the fumes from his own bullshit!

To add insult to injury he hasn't even turned to grace me with his attention. Well, fuck you with a giant fucking strap-on!

"Well, I hope you enjoyed the show Boss Man because I know for a fact every other man and most of the women did too. So, if you want to believe I crave your attention you can fuck right off, you delusional arsehole!"

I turn and walk towards the door ready to get the fuck out of here and forget I ever met this arsehole. Urgh! I don't even hear him approaching, before I'm twisted and he's pressing me to the wall in two seconds flat.

His chest is heaving, and his eyes are piercing right down to my soul. His body is pinning me to the wall and his hand is gripping my throat. Not hard enough to choke me, but the grip is punishing.

I should be scared and a small part of me is, but the bigger part of me is on fire. As in oh my God this is fucking panty-wetting hot. He's so big, so angry and so fucking hot I nearly fucking forget he's an arsehole. Nearly!

"You need to keep that smart mouth of yours shut, my Little Vixen, because you are pushing your luck now. Do not mention any other man or woman in my presence again. I don't give a fuck what you say anymore but you have got my attention. The whole twisted fucking lot of it. And you will not be escaping so easily, do you hear me? I will punish that sexy fucking arse of yours until you confess you are lying and tell me how much you like my attention! With the marks on your delectable arse to prove it and remind you for days!"

I think I would be a puddle on the floor if he didn't have me pinned to the wall. Fucking hell that was hot, I'm burning up and blushing like mad. This man is so infuriating! He's such a dickhead, then he says things like that which turn me on. I'm so confused, my mind and my body are at war.

"If you think that I will admit to wanting your attention, let alone liking it, you're more of an idiot than I thought!" I spit, peering at him through my lashes.

"We shall see then won't we, my Little Vixen?" He's staring down at me, with the threat beating down on my body like a storm ready to engulf me. His eyes are flicking from my eyes to my lips. Suddenly, I'm nervous about what he's going to do.

"Bring it on Boss Man!" Shit, the words come out before I can stop them. I glance up at him and go to say something else. Hell, I don't know, maybe even *'sorry Mr Boss Man'* but I don't get a chance to do anything as his lips come crashing down on mine.

I'm so shocked I freeze; I can do absolutely nothing until his tongue licks across my bottom lip, demanding access. I must suddenly be beyond reasonable thinking, because I open to him, giving him all the permission he needs. He starts off the kiss so softly, caressing my tongue with his, encouraging me to participate.

What Kai doesn't know, what no one knows as a matter of fact, aside from my best friend and secret bodyguard Luka, is that I've never been touched by a man like this, or more than this. Not even so much as a kiss! There were rules to my previous life and if anybody had touched a hair on my head, they would have been killed.

Believe me, I've had plenty of chances since I left but I just haven't wanted to. I put on a good act as the "sexy vixen" Kai keeps on calling me, but it's all a front. A mask per se, but I feel as if that mask has been ripped off and shredded in one fell swoop.

I melt into Kai and start to respond to the kiss as best I can. This seems to be the response he was waiting for because suddenly, the kiss goes from slow and sensual to wild and animalistic in seconds. All I can do is hold on to his shirt in a tight grip and cling on for the ride.

Kai

I swear I think this woman in my arms, or should I say pinned to the wall, is who I was thinking about when I named this club. She has enticed me with her Siren's call, and I have no control whatsoever.

I don't kiss at all, it's one of my fucking rules. No kissing, no dates, no details. Fuck all personal. It's a fuck or a blow job then fuck off, but this woman has me ripping up my rule book and wanting, for the first time, to call somebody MINE! What the ever-loving fuck!

I was kissing her softly, trying to encourage her to respond but when she did? All bets were off. A flip switched in me, and my inner beast came to the forefront and said fuck this shit.

I'm now fucking her mouth with my tongue, clashing teeth and desperately trying to put my claim on this woman for everybody to see. To my surprise, she's giving back as much as I'm giving her.

She starts to writhe in my hold and lets out little whimpers which are sexy as fuck. I want to consume her, own her, and mark her so deep she will never be able to deny my claim again.

My cock has only been interested in her since I first saw her on stage, even after I blew my load in that bitches mouth. It wanted her then and it wants her now. It's as insatiable for her as I am.

I break the kiss sharply, ripping my lips away from her and she lets out a whine in protest which shoots directly to my balls. Fucking hell this woman will be the death of me.

I grab her waist and lift her higher on the wall, pinning her with my body again. She squeaks, but then wraps her legs around my waist. This position puts her hot, wet, little pussy directly against my aching cock.

Her dress has luckily opened due to the high split, giving me access to those glorious silky thighs. Looking down I run my hands from her knees up to the top of her thighs. Before sliding my hands underneath and squeezing in a punishing grip.

I put my forehead against hers and try to take a breath while my cock is throbbing against her wet panties. I look into her eyes and see that she is just as fucked as I am. If this was death, we both welcomed it with open arms.

I lift my right hand and push a finger underneath the flimsy little strap holding up the dress on her shoulder. I let it fall and it slips off, revealing her right breast. Her breasts are fucking unbelievable; voluptuous, and pert. She has tight rosebud nipples, begging to be sucked within an inch of their life.

I groan, grinding my cock against her pussy and her back arches, pushing her breasts out and up. I can't resist. I lower my mouth to her rosebud nipple and suck hard. She mews and writhes in my hold but there's no escape. I can't help myself and I bite down hard on her nipple.

"Oh, Oh, please, oh God Kai, argh, YES!" I smile around my mouthful and give her breast a quick kiss, then bring my head back slightly to blow gently on her wet nipple.

Her hands come up and wind themselves in my

hair, scratching my scalp desperately with her nails, arching her back even more in an attempt to get me to put it back in my mouth.

"Oh, poor baby, is it a tease? Hmm… not getting the satisfaction that your body craves? You see, my beautiful Little Vixen, you have been a very naughty girl and naughty girls don't get rewarded. Naughty girls get punished, and if they are good girls taking it, they get rewarded."

To prove my point I grabbed her wet rosy nipple and twisted it hard. She screams and looks at me, panting with so much lust in her eyes it's beautiful. My Little Vixen likes pain with her pleasure. Fucking perfect.

I grip her under her thighs again and pull away from the wall, carrying her over to my chair, to sit down with her straddling my lap. She looks at me puzzled and starts to try and pull the strap back up on her dress. But I grab her wrist and squeeze slightly, raising my brow. She releases the strap, raising a brow in question back at me. I raise my finger and lightly circle her nipple. A whisper of touch to stimulate but leave her wanting more.

"Little Vixen, your performance earlier left me with quite a puzzling conclusion. If that performance were just for me in private it would have been appreciated greatly and rewarded accordingly. Both satisfactory to myself and you. As it is, you decided to give that little performance in front of the whole club. You let those men see what was meant for my eyes only and I can't let that misbehaviour go unpunished now, can I?"

Her brows crease and she seems to break out of the lust-filled bubble I had her in. She grabs my wrist to try and stop my touch on her. I grab her throat with my other hand and shake my head lightly, to tell her it's not going to happen.

"What the fuck are you on about Kai? It was a dance, it's what you pay me for. I dance in your club, not just for you!" She attempts to get off my lap, but I tighten my grip on her throat. Her eyes widen and she tries to swallow past my grip.

"That there, honey, was not just your normal performance. Believe me, I have seen hundreds. You wanted to play with the devil, and you gained his attention well and truly. Now that you have my undivided attention there is no escape. You will be mine to do what I want to when I want to. I will guarantee you one thing though, my Little Vixen, you will love every single depraved moment of it and beg for more!"

Her eyes are dilated and she's breathing heavily. She's conflicted, I can tell by the way her brows are drawn together. My Little Vixen is going to be more of a challenge than I anticipated, her submission will be hard-won but oh-so-delicious when she gives it to me.

"My name is Annabelle, Belle to my friends, but you

will never be one of those arsehole. One thing I can guarantee to you is that I will never be yours. No way in hell will a man own me, in this life or the next. You can go and get blondie back for round two because I'm not fucking interested!"

She tried again to get herself free from my grip, but she's got no chance. I'm not letting her go, and it's about time she learned; that when I've decided something, it's fucking final.

I flip her so quickly she doesn't have time to respond, so she's now lying across my lap. She's kicking and screaming profanities at me, which will only earn her more lashes on that delectable arse. I move my leg and trap both of her legs between mine, ripping her dress up as I do, to reveal her peachy arse in yet another thong. I growled deep from my chest, and tip her top half toward the floor, so she's forced to put her arms down to steady herself.

Undoing my belt buckle, I whip it out of my belt loops. She starts to renew her struggles as she must have heard the buckle being undone. No chance Little Vixen, you're mine now!

I put pressure on her lower back and lay my belt across her back. I start rubbing her arse cheeks and down the back of her thighs, then pick up my belt and double it over.

"Now my Little Vixen, each time I strike you with my belt you will count and thank me for your punishment. Then you will ask me nicely to have another. You will receive ten strikes, but only if you are a good girl and take your punishment correctly. If you misbehave or lose count, we will go back to the beginning and start again!"

She starts really struggling and screaming again. My Little Vixen is quite strong for her size and has so much feistiness, but all she's doing is delaying the inevitable.

"Argh, Kai, let me the fuck go you fucking lunatic. I swear I will punch you right in the fucking face if you dare raise that fucking belt to me. Argh KAI!"

I pin her with my legs and arm, then raise the belt and bring it right down on her left arse cheek, hard. She screamed and cried out for me to stop, but she isn't giving me the response I requested.

"I warned you before I started, Little Vixen, that I would not accept anything less than what I requested you to say. So shall we start again? If you want to be able to sit down in the next week, I suggest you think very carefully about your response after the next strike!"

She whimpers and struggles again but it will not deter me. I bring the next strike of my belt down hard on her left arse cheek. I was right before; her porcelain skin marks beautifully. My marks will last days for the world to see, which sends a flare of heat through my body. Mine!

"You better stop Kai or I will make sure you will regret every strike you bestow on me from now on!"

I strike her again, because she has a mouth on her that needs to be stopped. She just needs to utter the words I fucking need her to say.

"Argh, I don't really give a shit who you are Boss Man, I will walk into your room and slit your throat when you least expect it! Mark my words," she hisses at me.

Her response makes me want to bend her over the table, fist that beautiful red hair and fuck her raw from behind.

"Little Vixen, I have explained the response I require. I will not ask again; I will just carry on until I get my response!"

She is trembling in my arms, her anger seeping out in waves, which still doesn't deter me from my end game. I lick away any tears because I crave them. I bring the belt down again on the right arse cheek, just above the last mark.

"One, thank you for my punishment and please may I have another!" She says it so quietly I think I've imagined it, as she's also sniffling at the same time.

"Good girl, now louder next time and we can get your punishment over and get on to the pleasure!" I bring the belt down again on the other side.

"Two, thank you for my punishment and please may I have another!" She says it louder this time and with less venom in her voice.

I bring the belt down twice in quick succession

on her sit spots, right under her arse cheeks. She screams and wriggles, crying for a moment.

"Three, Four, thank you for my punishment and please may I have another!" I let out a loud growl and grip my belt tighter. I'm just about hanging on to my discipline here, as I just want to lift her up and place her on my throbbing cock. The pain of my erection against my fly is the best kind of agony.

I carry on the spanking and get the correct response every time. By the time we get to eight she lets out a moan.

"Does my Little Vixen enjoy my belt? I wonder, if I felt your pussy would it be soaked for me, Hmm? Shall I see?"

She moaned again and I draped my belt on her reddened arse. I ran my hand down her arse cheek slowly and dipped my fingers under her panties. I push my digits through her pussy lips and directly to her clit. Fucking hell, she's soaked. I laugh and continue, running small circles around her clit, not quite giving her any relief.

"Good girl, such a good girl for me. I think my Little Vixen likes my type of punishment. So I think that, if you are naughty in the future, I'll have to think up a different type of punishment for you!"

My Little Vixen lets out an agitated whine and tries to wriggle her pussy slightly to get me exactly where she wants relief. *Not yet baby, soon.* I remove my fingers from her pussy and put them in my mouth.

Fucking hell, she tastes amazing. The sweetest nectar I've ever tasted and now I just want her to sit on my face.

I hear her groan and look down to find her head slightly turned, watching me. I lick my fingers clean and pick up my belt again, giving her the last two strikes halfway down her thighs.

I quickly pick her up and place her straddling my lap again, she won't be able to sit properly for a while. I rub her arse and knead it occasionally, which makes her arch her back with a mix of pain and pleasure.

"Such a good girl, you are such a good fucking girl. I need to fuck you baby; I need to fuck your pussy right here and now!"

I move my hand around and dip my fingers into her pussy lips again. She moans and I move further back, towards her tight little hole. As I'm about to push in she grabs my hand and stops me. I look up and her face has gone from euphoria to worry in two seconds flat!

"What's wrong Annabelle?" I frown, looking directly into her eyes.

"I…" She tries to look away, but I grab her jaw and make sure she's looking straight into my eyes.

"Tell me what's the matter now, Annabelle!" She starts to blush and looks down.

"I can't Kai, I just can't!" She's got tears in her eyes and I'm starting to get worried now, and a little mad.

She will fucking answer me.

"Answer me now, Little Vixen, or I will be forced to punish you in another way which will be far less pleasurable for you I promise!"

Her teary eyes shoot to mine.

"I'm a fucking virgin you arsehole! Are you happy now?" She looks down again.

I'm fucking gobsmacked, that's the last thing I expected to come out of her mouth. Fucking hell, she's the sexiest fucking virgin I've ever met. All my thoughts race and I can see she's going further, back into her head. Fuck that!

"Fucking hell baby, you're so fucking hot it's unbelievable! You're coming home with me now!" I stand up with her in my arms and chuck her over my shoulder.

"Kai, what are you doing? Put me down right now!" She starts thumping my back.

"Baby, you're going nowhere except my fucking bed! There's no escape for you now, my Little Vixen!"

Chapter 3

Annabelle

"Put me down Kai, you can't carry me through the club like this! You fucking neanderthal, let me go!"

I scream and pound at his back with my fists. He will not carry me, like a stricken damsel in distress over his shoulder, like a prize he's won! I'm so mad right now, he better watch out if he lets me go at any point. I will show him who he's messing with.

He walks out the VIP lounge door and passes Lev. I lift my head up to find Lev smirking at me and following behind us.

"Lev, why the fuck are you amused? Will you tell him he's being ridiculous carrying me through the club like this!"

"I thought you were going to have him purring like a kitten Little Red, what's the matter? Did you deny him his cream?"

Lev tips his head back, chuckling, as I stick my swivel finger up at him, smiling maniacally.

"Okay Lev, you have now put yourself on my shit list.

I'm going to enjoy kicking you in the balls once I'm free!"

Why the hell did I think Lev would help me? He's loyal to Kai and how can I really blame him for that? Luka will always have my back and has done since I was a kid. Oh my God, Luka is going to flip his lid if I don't return tonight, I need to contact him but what the fuck am I going to tell him?

"Oh, I'm shaking in my boots Little Red. Can you see me shaking?" Lev chuckled, his smile breath-taking and sadistic at the same time. It's how it kicks up slightly further on the right-hand side than the left. The dimples deepen in his cheeks, giving him that lovable rogue look but his eyes show me his true self.

"Fuck you arsehole!"

We descend the stairs and Kai carries me past Greg and Peter, out into the main club. I look up at them both and Greg goes to step forward to do something, but Peter grabs his arm and pulls him back. All I see is their heated argument as I'm carried further into the main club.

As we pass the bar. I see Sam and her face is stricken. She runs up to Lev as we pass and they start arguing. Sam is a little firecracker, she's much smaller than Lev but is on her tiptoes trying to get in his face. Lev just grabs her hair and pulls her head back bending down to put them face to face. Sam seems to melt in his hold as he says something to her that I can't hear. Interesting!

Kai is still making his way out with me and I'm running out of time now. It looks like I'm not going to get any help. I start trying to kidney punch Kai to escape, but he's so bloody tall that I can't quite get an effective strike.

"Let me the fuck down, you psycho!"

I scream at the top of my lungs, hitting and kicking him as much as his hold on my thighs allows. He suddenly stops smack bang in the middle of the club and everyone is staring at us, waiting to see what's going to happen.

I start to think he's going to let me go and then I feel an almighty slap on my arse. It's like I've been electrocuted. The shock is astounding. My arse was painful enough with his lash marks still throbbing. This has ignited not only the pain of that experience, but also sent a bolt to my traitorous pussy.

"You will behave and be a good girl now Annabelle, or do you want to meet my belt again? Believe me, my Little Vixen, I will not hesitate to place you across my knee and paint your arse with more of my marks right here in the middle of my club!"

He's silent, awaiting my answer, as I expect the whole room is. I wouldn't know because I haven't lifted my head since he spanked me. I'm in a haze of embarrassment, lust, and confusion. I hate this man so much in this moment. He's so damn annoying, but I can't deny the way he makes me feel.

He takes my silence as my answer and starts to make his way out of the club again. I go limp in his hold. Let him think I've given up but I'm just saving my energy.

We make it outside and I shiver from the cold. Come on, it's Birmingham in the middle of March, it's freezing. At least it's not raining though.

Kai puts me down and grabs my arm, turning me to a car that's ready and waiting at the curb. Lev appears and opens the back door for us to enter. I've had enough of this shit now, so I go full attack mode and show these fuckers I'm not to be messed with.

Kai releases his hold on me and slips his arm around my waist to steer me into the back seat. As I get close enough to Lev, I strike as fast as I can. Grinning, I twist and knee Lev right in his bollocks, hard. He goes down to his knees, cupping his bollocks and I twist quickly to Kai. Who's staring at me in a mixture of astonishment and lust, but fuck you arsehole.

People have underestimated me all my life. I'm used to it. Kai goes to grab me, but I drop to the floor and avoid his reach. I flip my shoes off and kick out with my right leg to sweep his legs out from beneath him. The trouble is he's massive, and I was really fooling myself if I thought I was going to drop him on his arse. His knees give a little but he stays standing, staring at me with amusement until someone grabs me from behind.

I'm dragged up and pinned in a punishing hold by the arms. I look at Kai and the murderous look on his face scares me for the first time since I've been in his presence. He isn't looking at me though, he's looking at the person holding me.

"Lev, if you do not take your hands off her now, I'll put a fucking bullet in your brain!"

What the fuck? I'm so shocked at what Kai's just said, but the more worrying feeling is why I think it was so bloody hot. I'm panting and hot, and my pussy seems hotwired to the man in front of me. I should be trying to escape or plead for my release but I'm frozen, pulled in by the force of this man's orbit.

"Chill Kai, I'm taking my hands off her now!"

Lev releases my arms and I turn to face him and start stepping back slowly, putting distance between us. What I forget though is I'm backing myself straight into the devil himself until it's too late. My back collides into a wall of muscle and Kai's hand comes up to grab me around my throat.

Lev has his hands up in surrender, his eyes following Kai with concern. Kai's breath is ragged at my back and his body is pulsing with brutal energy. His anger is whirling around us all, threatening to engulf us and leave nobody in its wake.

Luckily, Sam decides at this precise moment to run out from the club with my bag gripped in her arms. She comes to a sudden stop, looking from me and

Kai to Lev. She looks worried and unsure whether to approach.

"It's okay Sam, come here sweetheart!" Lev says, not taking his eyes off Kai.

Kai's body seems to relax a bit behind me, but he doesn't release the punishing grip he has on my throat. He lowers his mouth down to my ear.

"Oh, my Little Vixen, you will pay for that little display, you really do love my punishments don't you baby? I will take it easier on you though because that was so fucking hot. I was thinking of tying you to my bed because I think you will look delectable, bound and gagged, waiting for my attention. I have now decided that I much prefer that fire and fight I just witnessed. When I get you into my bed Annabelle, I need you to give me your worst baby, show me your inner monster. I swear Little Vixen, we will have such a euphoric experience burning together on our way down to hell!"

I gasp and shudder as Kai straightens back up and pushes his engorged erection into my back. If I was on fire before I'm self-combusting now. He seems to have a hold over me that no other man has ever had. Not even my arsehole of a Papa.

I'm watching as Lev and Sam have yet another heated whispered discussion, and Lev tries to calm her by putting two fingers under her chin and raising her face to his. He's now forgotten about Kai's threat and is solely focused on Sam.

Kai turns me to face him, and I lift my eyes to his face automatically. He brushes my cheek with his palm and places a soft kiss on my forehead.

"Good girl, now I'm going to get you in the car, and I want you to be on your best behaviour. Lev will bring your bag from Sam, okay?"

"I'll come with you Kai, just don't hurt Sam, please!"

Sam has a little girl, and I don't want her getting hurt for interfering and trying to save me.

"Nobody will hurt anyone Annabelle, just get in the car okay!"

Kai opens the door and I get in, sinking into the luxurious seats. Kai shuts the door, goes around the other side and lowers himself into the seat next to me in the back.

I'm filled with nervous energy and worry. I look out the window to check on Sam. She's now standing hugging herself as Lev walks toward the car we're in. She averts her eyes from watching Lev's retreating figure to looking at me. We lock eyes and I give her a smile which I hope reassures her that I'm fine. She smiles tightly, but I know I'm not kidding her at all…

The story continues in The Siren's Call available now from Amazon and on Ku.

Author's Note

Thank you so much for reading A step into The Siren's Call, I hope you enjoyed the taster. You can find out what happens next in The Siren's Call. The Treasured Possession Duet is available now on Amazon, KU and at signings I'm partaking in. Book 1 is The Siren's Call and Book 2 is Nikolai's Vixen. The Vixen's and Vendetta's series then continues with the next duet The Delicate Possession duet coming soon.

I always appreciate your feedback and would be grateful if you could leave me a review on Amazon, Goodreads or social media.

As with all Authors, reviews mean the world to us. They encourage us to strive for more, help us when we are low, and tell us that you love the worlds we create for you.

About Tammy

Tammy Bradley lives in England with her Fiancé, Craig, the love of her life and her children. She is the mother of four beautiful girlies; her family means the world to her. She has a crazy Chihuahua and a psycho budgie. She loves a good cuppa, chocolate and sweets. Reading is her main passion along with her love of films. She loves Marvel and Transformers with a nerdy obsession, with Quick Silver and Bumblebee being amoung her favourite characters of all time.

Tammy loved stories and writing as a child, and would often spend time alone with a book or writing pad. She left this behind as she grew up, worked, and started her family with Craig. After a tragic loss in the family, her eldest daughter brought her The Mortal Instruments book set as a gift. The love of reading returned and offered an escape from the devastation.

Hundreds of books later, she finally admitted to her family that her life's ambition had always been to become an Author, but her self-doubt had always stood in the way.

As they say the rest is history, and now Tammy writes dark romance books. Her first book The Siren's Call is part of The Treasured Possessions duet, a dark mafia romance. This is just the start of her journey; she invites you to come along and enjoy the ride.

Connect with Tammy

Join Tammy on social media. She regularly posts about updates and her next books on TikTok, Facebook and Instagram.

Join Tammy on Facebook

Author Tammy Bradley official fan group – All Sorts

Join Tammy on Tiktok

@authortammybradley

Join Tammy on Instagram

@authortammybradley

You can also subscribe to Tammy's newsletter through her website.

www.AuthorTammyBradley.com

Printed in Dunstable, United Kingdom